ELMO'S First Babysitter

By Sarah Albee
Illustrated by Tom Brannon

Dalmatian Press, LLC, 2006. All rights reserved.
Published by Dalmatian Press, LLC, 2006. The DALMATIAN PRESS name and logo are trademarks of Dalmatian Press, LLC, Franklin, Tennessee 37067. No part of this book may be reproduced or copied in any form without written permission from the copyright owner.

Printed in the U.S.A.
ISBN: 1-40373-027-X (T)

06 07 08 09 NGS 10 9 8 7 6 5 4 3 2
15425 Sesame Street 8x8 Storybook: Elmo's First Babysitter

Elmo is so excited! Elmo is going to have a babysitter tonight! Her name is Emily. There's the doorbell! That must be Emily!

Um, wait a minute. Maybe Elmo doesn't really want a babysitter after all.

It *is* Emily. She looks nice, doesn't she? Elmo's mommy and daddy wrote down the phone number of the place they're going tonight. And they also wrote the phone numbers of our neighbors, just in case. Now it's time to hug Mommy and Daddy good-bye.

Did you see what we made? Kooky faces! Elmo made this one all by himself!

Wow! Elmo likes this music!

Elmo's toe feels all better now. And look—Emily
brought bubbles for Elmo to play with in the bathtub.
When Mommy and Daddy give Elmo a bath, we don't
ever get to blow bubbles.

Good morning, Mommy! Good morning, Daddy!
Elmo liked having a babysitter! It was fun!
When is Emily coming back?